www.BillieBBrownBooks.com

Billie B. Brown Books

The Bad Butterfly
The Soccer Star
The Midnight Feast
The Second-best Friend
The Extra-special Helper
The Beautiful Haircut
The Big Sister
The Spotty Vacation
The Birthday Mix-up
The Secret Message
The Little Lie
The Best Project

First American Edition 2013
Kane Miller, A Division of EDC Publishing

Text copyright © 2010 Sally Rippin
Illustrations copyright © 2010 Aki Fukuoka
Logo and design copyright © 2010 Hardie Grant Egmont

First published in Australia in 2010 by Hardie Grant Egmont

For information contact:
Kane Miller, A Division of EDC Publishing
P.O. Box 470663
Tulsa, OK 74147-0663
www.kanemiller.com
www.edcpub.com
www.usbornebooksandmore.com

Library of Congress Control Number: 2011935696

Printed and bound in the United States of America
2 3 4 5 6 7 8 9 10
ISBN: 978-1-61067-098-2

The Second-best Friend

By Sally Rippin

Illustrated by Aki Fukuoka

Kane Miller
A DIVISION OF EDC PUBLISHING

Chapter One

Billie B. Brown has six sparkly pens, three blisters on her hands and one best friend. Do you want to know what the "B" in Billie B. Brown is for?

Best.

Billie's best friend is Jack.

Do you know how long Billie and Jack have been friends? Since they were babies.

Now that Billie and Jack are big, they go to school. Every day they walk to school together.

Three blisters

Six sparkly pens

3

Every day they walk
home together. Every day
they sit next to each
other in class.

Today Billie has decided
to take her new pens
to school.

Jack gave Billie the sparkly pens for her birthday. The sparkly pens write in sparkly ink, and they smell like fruit. Billie loves her new pens.

Billie puts her pens on the desk. She takes out a pink pen and pulls off the cap. Soon the whole classroom smells like strawberries.

"Hmm," says Ms. Walton,
wrinkling up her nose.
"Is someone eating?"

Everyone in the room stops working and looks around. Billie quickly puts the cap back on her pen. She is **worried** that she might get in trouble.

"Billie?" says Ms. Walton, frowning. "Have you brought candy to school?"

"No!" says Billie quickly. "It's my sparkly pen."

"Oh," says Ms. Walton, smiling. "My goodness, it smells strong, doesn't it?"

"Can I see?" Ella calls, jumping up from her desk.

"Me too!" calls Tracey from her seat next to Ella.

"Now, girls," Ms. Walton says. "Sit down. You can all look at Billie's pens at lunchtime."

Billie feels very proud. She looks at Jack. He smiles at Billie.

When the bell goes, the girls crowd around Billie to look at her new pens.

"Where did you get them?" Lola asks.

"Jack gave them to me," Billie says. "For my birthday."

"Ooh, Jack!" Lola teases. "Your boyfriend!"

"He's not my boyfriend," says Billie, frowning. "That's just silly!"

"Yes, he is," Lola grins.

"He's a boy. And he's your friend. That makes him your *boyfriend*."

The other girls giggle.

Billie frowns. Sometimes Lola and her friends can be so annoying!

Chapter Two

Billie and Jack walk
over to the monkey bars.
They climb up to the top
to eat their lunch.
After they have eaten,
they practice hanging

upside down to see who can last the longest.

The bell rings. Billie and Jack walk back to class.

Just then, Rebecca walks
up to Billie. Rebecca is in
Billie and Jack's class.
She has long, shiny braids

with ribbons in them. Billie would love to have long, shiny braids like Rebecca's. Billie stops. Jack runs ahead.

Rebecca has something in her hands. It is a purple pony. Billie feels a teensy bit **jealous**.

Rebecca always has the best toys for Show and Tell.

"Cool pony," Billie says.

"Thanks," Rebecca says. "Do you want a turn?"

Billie puts out her hand. Rebecca gives her the pony. It's beautiful. Billie wishes she had a pony like that.

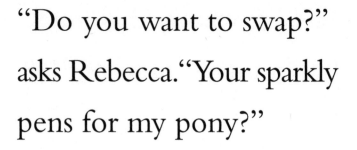

"Do you want to swap?" asks Rebecca. "Your sparkly pens for my pony?"

"Oh!" says Billie. She doesn't know what to do. She loves the purple pony. But the sparkly pens were a present from Jack. Would he get **mad** if she swapped them?

"I don't know," Billie says.
She feels all **muddled**.

"You can come to my house and play with my other toys too," Rebecca says. "I have heaps more ponies. And we could do your hair in braids like mine."

Billie looks at the little purple pony. She looks at Rebecca's long, shiny braids. She would love to have the pony.

She would love to have hair like Rebecca's. Most of all, she would love to be Rebecca's friend.

"Um, OK!" says Billie.

She gives Rebecca the pens and slips the pony into her pocket. Then she and Rebecca run back to class.

Billie feels so **excited**
that her tummy is
jumping around like a
little fish.

Chapter Three

At the end of the day,
Billie and Jack walk to
the front gate together.
But today Rebecca
is there. She is waiting
for Billie.

Rebecca's and Billie's moms are talking.

"Hi, Billie!" calls Rebecca. "Your mom says you can come over."

"Today?" says Billie.

"But what about our fort?" Jack says to Billie.

"Billie doesn't have to always play with you," Rebecca says.

Billie looks at Jack. She can see that Jack looks **upset**, but she doesn't know what to say. She mainly feels **excited** that Rebecca wants to be her friend.

"We can finish the fort another time, Jack," she says quietly.

Jack frowns and looks down at his sneakers.

"Come on, Billie," Rebecca says. "My mom's waiting!"

Billie follows Rebecca to her car. She waves to Jack, but he is still looking at the ground.

Billie and Rebecca sit in the back seat. Billie feels **excited**. She has a new toy pony and a new friend.

But then Billie thinks
about Jack and feels
bad. The bad feeling
makes her tummy twist
up inside.

Chapter  Four

Soon they arrive. Rebecca's house is big and white like a cake. Her bedroom is pink and purple, and it has more toys than Billie has ever seen.

Billie watches Rebecca take the sparkly pens out of her school bag and put them on her desk.
When Billie sees the sparkly pens, her tummy squeezes tight.

Rebecca's dad has bought cupcakes for afternoon tea. The cupcakes have little faces on them.

They are sugary and soft,
not like the oatmeal bars
that Billie's mom makes.

"Have another, Billie!"
Rebecca's mom says.

Billie wants to eat
another cupcake, but her
tummy is feeling **funny**.
She drinks some juice,
but it doesn't make her
feel better.

"I don't feel well," Billie
says in a small voice.

"Oh dear," says Rebecca's mom. She puts her hand on Billie's forehead. "That's all right. I can take you home. Why don't you choose a cupcake to take with you?"

Rebecca's mom wraps a cupcake in a pink paper napkin.

"You girls go upstairs to get Billie's things," she says.

Billie and Rebecca walk upstairs. Billie knows what she has to do to feel better.

She takes the little pony out of her pocket. Even though it is the nicest pony Billie has ever had,

she knows that she can't
keep it. She holds it out
to Rebecca.

"I'm sorry," she says.
"Can we swap back
again? My friend gave
me those sparkly pens.

He'll be sad if he finds out I gave them away."

"I know why you want them back," Rebecca says. She hands the pens back to Billie. "They're from your boyfriend."

"Jack is not my boyfriend!" Billie says crossly. "He's my friend.

My *best* friend. He's the bestest best friend around!" Billie thinks of Jack and smiles. "He's funny, and he's good on the monkey bars, and he's really good at making forts too. He can make a fort just from sticks and leaves!"

"Wow!" Rebecca says.

"I'm not allowed to make forts in our backyard. Mom says they make too much mess."

"You should come and play in our fort then," Billie says, smiling. "I'm sure Jack won't mind. There's lots of room!"

"Really? Thanks, Billie!"
says Rebecca.

"Billie?" Rebecca's mom
calls. "Are you ready?"

"Coming!" Billie shouts. She grabs her school bag and shoves the pens into the front pocket.

"Wait!" says Rebecca. She grabs Billie's hand. "Keep the pony."

"Why?" asks Billie, feeling **worried**. "Don't you want to swap back?"

"It's not that. I've got lots of pens," Rebecca says. "I've got lots of toy ponies too. But I don't have any friends like you, Billie. You can keep the pony."

"Thanks!" Billie says **happily**. Then she has an idea. "Maybe we could be second-best friends?"

"Cool!" says Rebecca.
"I'd like that!"

"Me too," says Billie.

Rebecca and Billie run downstairs.

Rebecca's mom starts the car. Rebecca waves goodbye to Billie.

Billie leans back against the car seat. Her tummy isn't hurting so much now. She takes the paper napkin out of her pocket and unwraps it.

The cupcake inside is a little bit squished, but she knows Jack will still like it.